Pesters of the West

Lisa Taylor and Tony Blundell

Collins
An *imprint of* HarperCollins*Publishers*

Look out for more *Jets* from Collins

First published by A & C Black Ltd in 1989
Published by Collins in 1989
10 9 8 7 6
Collins is an imprint of HarperCollins*Publishers*Ltd,
77–85 Fulham Palace Road, Hammersmith, London W6 8JB

ISBN 0 00 673345 X

Text © Lisa Taylor 1989
Illustrations © Tony Blundell 1989

The author and the illustrator assert the moral right to
be identified as the author and the illustrator of the work.
A CIP record for this title is available from the British Library.
Printed and bound in Great Britain by
Caledonian International Book Manufacturing Ltd, Glasgow

Meet Esther and Hester Pester.

Esther and Hester are twins.
They have
1) Big gappy teeth with braces.

2) Ears they can waggle up and down

3) Hair which grows upwards instead of downwards and makes them look like they are about to take off.

Esther and Hester are prize peashooting champions.

4

Meet Ma Pester.

Ma Pester is Esther and Hester's mother. She is big and strong and looks like a pudding with a chuckly face. Her hobbies include baking and bowling pumpkin dumplings.

Meet Sylvester Pester.

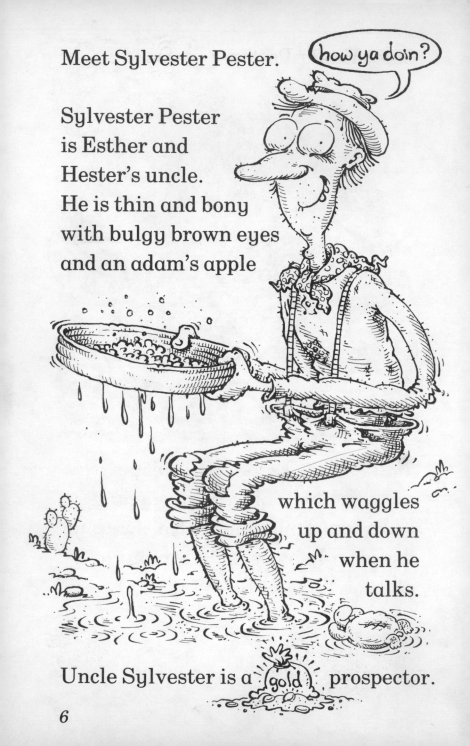

Sylvester Pester
is Esther and
Hester's uncle.
He is thin and bony
with bulgy brown eyes
and an adam's apple

which waggles
up and down
when he
talks.

Uncle Sylvester is a gold prospector.

Meet Fester Pester.

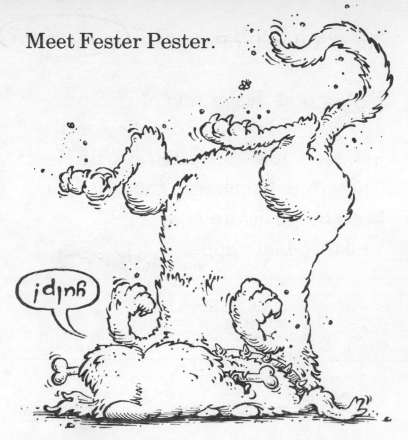

Fester Pester is Esther and Hester's dog. He likes chewy sticks, squeaky bones and rolling in things which are smelly.

Chapter One

Esther and Hester and Ma Pester
and Uncle Sylvester and Fester live
in Chipmunk Creek in the Wild West.
Chipmunk Creek is in the middle of
the state of Colorado.

Esther and Hester think it is in the
middle of nowhere.

It was never wild in Chipmunk Creek.

There were
no goodies
to cheer for,

no baddies
to boo,

no broncos
to buck,

no cows
to lassoo.

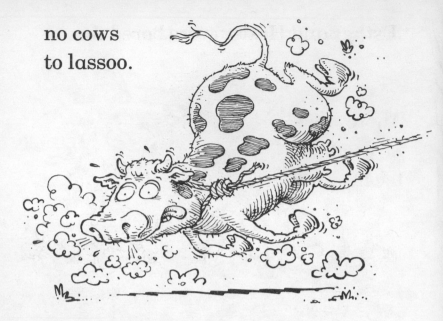

There wasn't even a chipmunk in
Chipmunk Creek!

All the chipmunks had left because
they were so bored.

Esther and Hester were bored too.

Every day in Chipmunk Creek was
the same as every other. Fester rolled,
Ma Pester bowled, and Uncle Sylvester
hunted for gold in the creek.
And Esther and Hester practised
hitting tin cans with their peashooters.

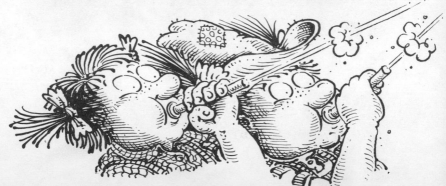

They were now so good
that they could hit
a moving tin can
with a
cannonball
pea

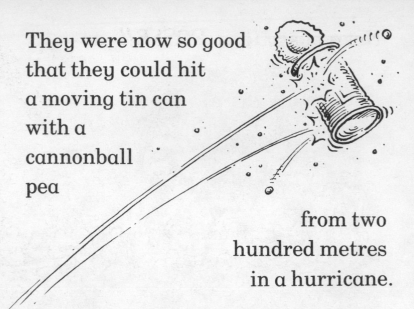

from two
hundred metres
in a hurricane.

Then one day – when Esther and
Hester were about to peashoot the
weather cock off the town hall roof –
a posse rode into town.

Not a *pussy* . . . a *POSSE!!*

Twelve angry-looking men and women
with ten-gallon hats and spiky
spurs and legs that were
shaped like a horse shoe.

'There's a bank robber escaped from Denver Jail,' said an angry-looking marshal.

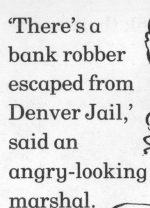

'Looks like he's headed up this way,' said an angry-looking deputy.

'Reckon he's buried some loot here,' said another angry-looking deputy.
'Seen anyone suspicious round these parts?'

Esther and Hester shook their heads.

'There's a mighty big reward,'
said the first angry-looking deputy.
'Ten thousand dollars for anyone
who brings him in alive!'

'What does he look like?'
asked Esther.

So the angry-looking marshal
showed them a picture.

'Why is he called Burnt Bottom
Bert?' asked Hester.

'Because he once sat on his own
branding iron,' said the marshal.

'Now he's got the letter 'B' branded on his bottom!'

And with that the marshal and the posse rode angrily away.

A big fat baddy! Bang in the middle of Chipmunk Creek! Esther and Hester whizzed home to tell their ma.

Chapter Two

While Esther and Hester were
talking to the posse, Uncle Sylvester
was singing and splashing
about in the creek. He was having
a happy time hunting for gold.

The sun was getting so hot that
Uncle Sylvester decided to give up
gold-hunting and go for a swim. He
put on his arm bands and waded into the creek.

Just as he got to the shivery bit
which came up to his tummy,
Uncle Sylvester noticed something
bobbing about in the middle
of the water.

At first he thought
it was a very
strange stick.

Next he thought
it was a rather
unusual fish.

Finally Uncle Sylvester swam over
to see what it was for himself.

The closer he got, the better he saw
that whatever it was – it was more
than one thing. Altogether Uncle
Sylvester counted *four* things
bobbing about – and all of them
were starting to sink. Uncle
Sylvester held his nose,

took a

deep

breath

and

dived

under

the

water.

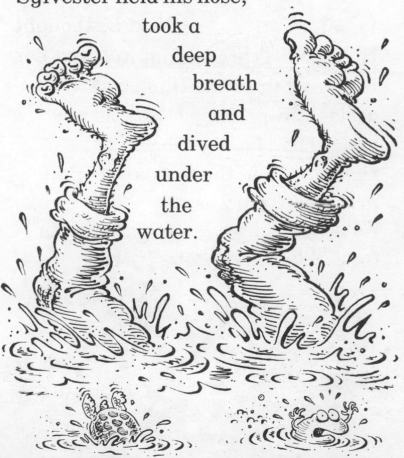

He grabbed three things in one hand and the other thing got accidentally wrapped around his head. Then he swam back to the shore and laid the things out on the ground. There was

1) A shirt.

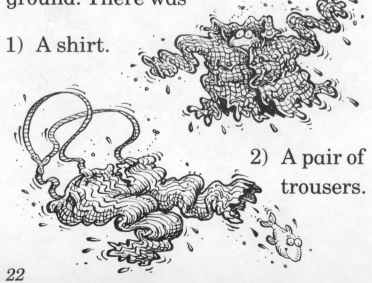

2) A pair of trousers.

3) A particularly pongy pair of socks.

Uncle Sylvester looked inside each thing. He found a name tag with large joined-up writing. It spelt the words

Burnt Bottom Bert

'Mighty strange place for folks to leave their clothes!' said Uncle Sylvester. 'Think I'll ask Ma Pester if she knows who he is.'

Chapter Three

Ma Pester was in the middle of
baking a pumpkin dumpling ready
for bowling the next day, when
Esther and Hester and Uncle
Sylvester all arrived at exactly the
same time.

'There's a
bankrobber loose
in Chipmunk Creek!'
yelled Esther.

'There's a ten thousand dollar reward!' yelled Hester.

'Does anyone know a Burnt Bottom Bert?' asked Uncle Sylvester.

'BURNT BOTTOM BERT!'

cried Esther and Hester.

'Yes,' replied Uncle Sylvester. 'Because I want to return his clothes.'

And Uncle Sylvester dumped them
on the table.

Esther and Hester examined
the clothes.

'Lôôk!' cried Esther.

'These clothes belong to the
bankrobber!' cried Hester.

'Well I'll be hornswoggled!'
said Uncle Sylvester.

'This can only mean one of two things,' said Esther.

'Either Burnt Bottom Bert is walking around in his underwear . . .'
said Hester.

'Or he is in disguise!'

Esther and Hester closed their eyes tight shut and tried

to imagine what sorts of disguises he might use.

'We're going into town to hunt him down,' said Esther and Hester.

'You won't catch him,' said Ma Pester.

'Probably in Nebraska by now,' said Uncle Sylvester.

But Esther and Hester were determined to look all the same.

Chapter Four

The first person that Esther and
Hester saw was a man with
a large hat,

a long beard,

and a big baggy
sack over his shoulder.

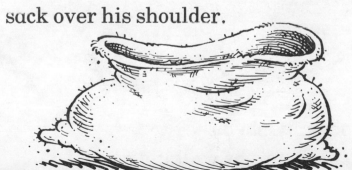

He was walking up to all the houses
looking very suspicious.

'It must be Burnt Bottom Bert in
disguise,' whispered Esther.

So Esther and Hester got into the
nearest dustbin

and ambushed the
man as he was walking past.

Esther pea-shooted off his hat and
jumped on his back so that she could
look inside his bag

and Hester jumped
on his beard and swung around on it
to see if it would come off.

It wouldn't.

And all Esther could find inside the
bag were piles and piles of letters.

Quick as a flash Esther and Hester
scooted off and dodged into the
nearest shop. They watched through
the window as the postman went
racing past.

Inside the shop there were rows and
rows of silly frilly posh frocks.

Round the corner,
Esther and Hester could
hear some people talking.
There was a large black
shadow on the wall.
Esther and Hester
stared at the shadow
in disbelief. It looked
like a man with a nose
the size of a prize
marrow!

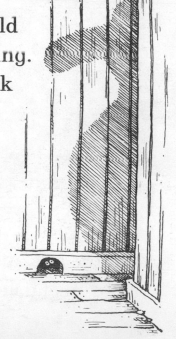

'It must be Burnt Bottom Bert in disguise,' whispered Hester.

With a great ROAR, Esther and Hester shot round the corner and pounced on what they thought was Burnt Bottom Bert's false nose. But the shadow they had seen turned out to be only half a shadow.

And the false nose turned out to be the brim of a very wide hat.

And the very wide hat turned out to be sitting on top of the Lady Mayoress's head.

The Lady Mayoress let out an enormous scream,

and
Esther
and
Hester
disappeared in a flurry of frilly frocks.

Chapter Five

Esther and Hester went home and
sat down and thought hard. Through
the window they could see
Fester . . .

. . . rolling in something extra smelly.

'I know!' cried Esther.

'We'll use Fester
as a tracker dog!'
cried Hester.

Esther and Hester whistled to Fester
and stuffed Burnt Bottom Bert's
socks under his nose for sniffing.

They had to wait five minutes for
him to recover from the pong.

The idea was that Fester would follow the scent from the socks and track Burnt Bottom Bert down. And Esther and Hester would follow Fester – wherever he went . . .

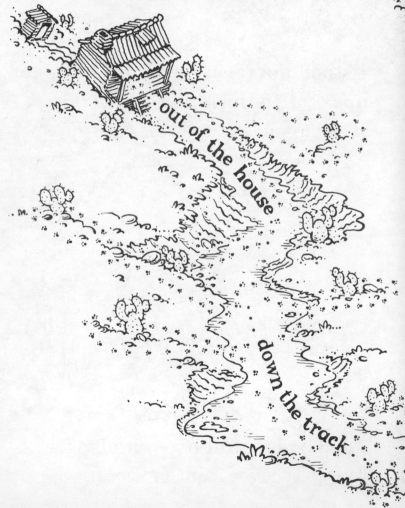

out of the house

down the track

when suddenly . . . WHOOOO

He disappeared
down one hole . . .

into the creek . . .

across the prairie . . .

SOOOSH! . . . and came back out of another hole chasing a skunk

The pong from the skunk was so strong that it smelt exactly like Burnt Bottom Bert's stinky socks!

Chapter Six

Holding their noses Esther and Hester
headed for home. Uncle Sylvester
was waiting for them. He was looking
all moony and starry-eyed.

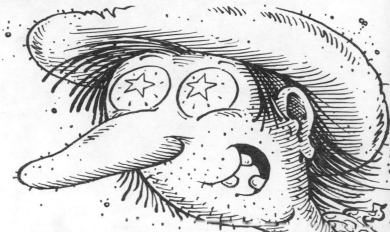

'I've met the most wonderful,
beautiful, charming woman in the
world,' sighed Uncle Sylvester,
'and I've asked her to marry me!'

'When?' cried Esther and Hester.

'Next Saturday,' replied
Uncle Sylvester.

'I want it to be the best day of my
life,' continued Uncle Sylvester.
'Lots of singing,

and dancing,

and flowers,
and most of all I want you both to be
the bridesmaids!'

Esther and Hester were horrified.

Flowers and frills and pink things
and perfumes! They preferred
to wear things which smelt
of buffalo dung.

'But we can't,' wailed Esther.

'We've got to find Burnt Bottom
Bert,' wailed Hester.

'And besides . . .' wailed Esther.

'We haven't even met the
bride,' wailed Hester.

So Ma Pester invited
her round for
some blueberry
pie.

Chapter Seven

The first time Esther and Hester
met Uncle Sylvester's bride-to-be,
their eyes went all round and
boggly – as if they had just sat down
on a prickly cactus.

Alberta Bottomley was like no
other woman they had ever seen
before. She was a head taller than
Uncle Sylvester and at least ten
heads wider with a face like an ugly
ogre, great slobbery chops and
horrible hairy nose tufts.

And she had a voice
which sounded like

But Uncle Sylvester liked her.
He said it didn't matter what people
looked like.

'Alberta is a very kind person,'
he said. 'She has already offered to
look after all my gold.'

But no matter what anyone said,
Esther and Hester didn't like her. It
wasn't just because they couldn't
hunt for Burnt Bottom Bert any
more. There was also something
rather odd about Alberta. For one
thing her bosoms kept changing
places . . .

Sometimes they were under her chin,

sometimes they were on her tummy,

and once they even went round her back.

Then there was her hair. It had a label coming out the side which said 100% nylon.

And her voice. Sometimes it sounded like a high burp and sometimes it sounded like a low **burp** .

And last of all her chin. It went all blue at about five o'clock in the afternoon.

Then Alberta would disappear and after a few scratchy noises she would come back and the blue had gone.

Esther and Hester got the feeling that there was more to Alberta Bottomley than met their boggly eyes.

Chapter Eight

Now Esther and Hester had no time
at all to look for Burnt Bottom Bert.
They had to be measured for their
dresses, choose their flowers,

POISON IVY   CACTUS   TUMBLE WEED   SELF RAISING

and try on little spangled shoes.

'Burnt Bottom Bert will be over the other side of the world by now,' they moaned.

When the wedding day arrived Esther and Hester howled and scowled and put on their frilly pink dresses. Then they had flowers piled on top of their hair.

They looked like two garden shrubs.

Esther and Hester got into a large white car which drove them to the church. On the way everyone waved and cheered and said how lovely the bridesmaids looked.

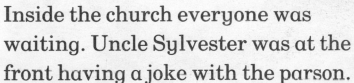

Inside the church everyone was waiting. Uncle Sylvester was at the front having a joke with the parson.

Quick-fingered Rick started playing
the Wedding March. Everyone held
their breath and Alberta Bottomley
came marching
up the aisle.

She wore a white dress and a large
veil to cover up her nose tufts. On
the back of the dress there was a big
bustle and a long wedding train.

Esther and Hester were fighting
over who should be carrying it. At
the same time they were waggling
their ears for uglification. Everyone
sat down and the ceremony began.

By this time the hustle over the
bustle was getting worse. It started

off as a quiet jostle ...turned into a bit of a scuffle ...became a much louder tussle and ended up as a huge rough and tumble.

Meanwhile the parson was trying to read the wedding vows.

'Do you Sylvester Pester take this woman to be your wedded wife?'

I do...

'I do,' said Uncle Sylvester dreamily.

'Do you Alberta Bottomley take this man to be your wedded husband?'

I do

'I do,' said Alberta sounding as if she had burped.

'Then I now pronounce you man and . . .'

RRRR

'Whatever's going on?' said the parson. For Esther and Hester had fallen flat over backwards and pulled the bustle and the wedding train completely off.

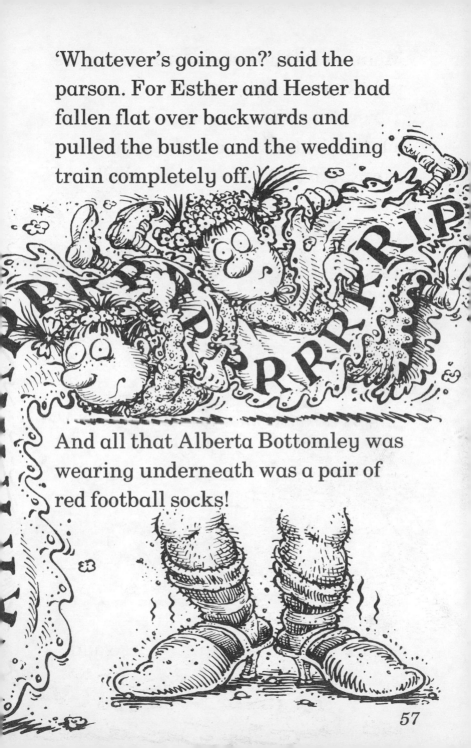

And all that Alberta Bottomley was wearing underneath was a pair of red football socks!

Chapter Nine

Everyone gasped in horror. And the more they looked the more they gasped. For not only did the bride have legs like a furry fuzz-ball, she also had the letter 'B' branded on her bottom!

Suddenly Esther and Hester realised what it was that was so odd about Alberta Bottomley.

'It's Burnt Bottom Bert the bankrobber,' they shouted, 'in disguise!'

Just as Burnt Bottom Bert was about to make a run for it, Esther and Hester took out their pea-shooters and fired two mighty cannonball peas.

At the same time Ma Pester
grabbed a huge dumpling which
she had wrapped up as a wedding
present

and bowled it down the aisle.

SPLAT! went the peas as they
knocked Burnt Bottom Bert's wig
over his face so that he couldn't see.

WHAM! went the dumpling as it
bowled him over like a skittle.

CRASH! went Burnt Bottom Bert
as he came tumbling to the floor.

Burnt Bottom Bert lay propped against
a pew with his eyes swivelling round
like a pinball machine. His wig had
fallen off and was lying on the floor.
There was an old piece of paper
tucked inside it.

Esther and Hester pounced on the
paper and started to wrestle over it.
So Ma Pester snatched it away . . .

'No wonder Burnt Bottom Bert was
getting married,' cried Ma Pester.
'He's buried some loot below Uncle
Sylvester's outhouse – right
underneath the toilet!'

'All this time,' said Uncle Sylvester sadly. 'I've been sitting on a fortune!'